Anna Sewell's
The Adventures of Black Beauty

Black Beauty Grows Up

8806

Adapted by I. M. Richardson
Illustrated by Karen Milone

Troll Associates

Library of Congress Cataloging in Publication Data

Richardson, I. M.
  Black Beauty grows up.

  (Anna Sewell's The adventures of Black Beauty; bk. 1)
  Summary: Black Beauty describes his early memories;
his experiences with his kind master, Squire Gordon;
and his sale to one of the squire's old friends.
    1. Horses—Juvenile fiction. [1. Horses—Fiction]
I. Milone, Karen, ill. II. Sewell, Anna, 1820-1878.
Black Beauty. III. Title. IV. Series: Richardson, I. M.
Anna Sewell's The adventures of Black Beauty; bk. 1.
PZ10.3.R413An bk. 1   [Fic]   82-7075
ISBN 0-89375-810-8   AACR2
ISBN 0-89375-811-6 (pbk.)

The first place I remember was a lovely meadow next to a plowed field. In the daytime, I ran by my mother's side, and at night, I lay down next to her. She gave me milk until I was old enough to eat grass. There were six other colts in the meadow besides me. But my mother said they were not as well bred as I was.

Our master was a kind man who took good care of us. One day he saw the plowboy throwing sticks and trying to make us gallop off.

"You bad boy!" he cried. Then he grabbed the boy by the collar and said, "Now go home, and don't come back here! I won't have you on my farm again."

My master said that colts should not work like horses until they were grown up. He refused to sell me until I was four years old. Then a man named Squire Gordon, who lived nearby, came and watched me for a long time. I heard him tell my master, "When he has been broken in, he will do very well." And my master said that he himself would do the breaking in.

"Breaking in" means teaching a horse to wear a bridle, bit, and saddle, and to carry a rider. It also means learning to pull a carriage or cart, and to do just what the driver wants you to do. My master was very gentle, so I quickly learned what he expected of me. I also learned not to shy away from things like trains or dogs or other horses.

After I was broken in, I was taken to Squire Gordon's stable. In the next stall was a gray pony whose name was Merrylegs. Next to him was a chestnut mare called Ginger. The coachman fitted me with a bridle and saddle, and took me out for a ride. His name was John Manly, and he was a kind and gentle man who loved horses.

The next day, the Squire rode me for the first time. He told his wife that he thought I was a fine horse. Then he said, "What shall we call him?" My mistress replied, "Why not Blackbird?" But my master said, "He's handsomer than any old blackbird." "Yes," agreed my mistress, "he is a beauty. Let's call him Black Beauty."

A few days later, Ginger and I were to pull the carriage. Before the Squire bought her, Ginger had lived a hard life. The men who broke her in had been too rough. They had whipped and beaten her. She had quickly learned not to trust people. But now she was slowly learning not to bite and kick. I soon found that she willingly did her share of the work.

Merrylegs was as gentle and good-natured as any pony could ever be. When the minister's children came to visit, they would ride him in circles, around and around the meadow. Even when he was so tired that he could go no more, Merrylegs never bit or kicked. Instead, he would just rear up on his hind legs, and let the children slide off safely.

One rainy day, John hitched me up to a one-horse carriage.
He was to drive the Squire into town on business. The man at
the wooden toll bridge said that the river was rising fast.
Some of the meadows were already flooded, and the water was
halfway up to my knees. By the time we reached town, the wind
had begun to blow very hard.

It was late when we started home. As we passed through the woods, the Squire told John that he had never been out in such a bad storm. Suddenly, there was a groan, and a crashing sound, and a huge tree fell across the road right in front of us! We could not go around it, so we had to turn back and take a different road to the toll bridge.

It was nearly dark by the time we reached the bridge. The river was so high that the middle of the bridge was now under water. I had scarcely started across when I stopped in my tracks. Something was wrong. "Go on, Beauty," urged John. But I would not move. The tollkeeper cried out, "The middle of the bridge has been washed away! You can't cross here!"

So we had to turn back again. We followed a road along the riverside, and arrived home well after dark. When my mistress heard the carriage, she ran out, calling, "Did you have an accident?" And the Squire said, "No, my dear. But if Black Beauty had not been wiser than we were, all of us might have been swept away in the river."

One day, as John and I returned from an errand, we came upon a boy who was cruelly whipping his pony. He was trying to make him jump over a gate that was too high for him. Suddenly, the pony kicked up his heels and threw the boy into a thorny hedge. "Help!" cried the boy. But John said, "Help yourself! Maybe a few thorns will teach you some kindness and sense."

Our stable boy was a young man named James Howard. He was a great help to John, and he knew how to take good care of the horses. We all liked him very much. One day, the Squire came into the stable and said, "Tell me, John. Is young James a good worker?" John replied, "Yes, sir. He's hard-working, honest, and smart." The Squire replied, "I thought as much."

Then the Squire said to James, "Mrs. Gordon's brother is looking for a young man to be his groom and driver. This is an excellent opportunity, and I wouldn't want to stand in your way. So think about it, and let me know what you decide." Soon it was settled that James would leave for his new job in six weeks.

18

James was already a very good groom, but he had little experience as a driver. Over the next few weeks, however, he got plenty of practice. Ginger and I were hitched to the carriage and taken out at every opportunity. At first, John went out with James, and taught him what to do and when to do it. But after that, James handled us all by himself.

Presently, my master and mistress decided to visit some friends who lived a distance away. James was to drive them, and Ginger and I would draw the carriage. The first day, we traveled more than halfway there. The roads were hilly and rutted, but James kept our feet on the smoothest part, and let us stop when we needed a moment's rest. At dusk, we reached a hotel.

Ginger and I were unhitched and led into a long stable. There were two or three other horses inside already. A friendly old man put me into a stall and rubbed me down as James looked on. Then Ginger and I were given our feed, and bedded down safely for the night. Finally, James went outside, and we went to sleep.

When I awoke, the stable was on fire! Someone burst in and untied the horses, but we were too frightened to follow him out. A moment later, James and another man came in quietly, and began soothing us. James tied his handkerchief over my eyes and led me outside. Then he went back in for Ginger. That was a night I will not soon forget!

The rest of our journey was easy. Around sunset, we got to the home of the Squire's friend. My master and mistress went inside, and Ginger and I were taken to the stable. When the coachman heard about the fire, he said to James, "Those horses must really trust you. In most stable fires, the horses are so scared that no one can get them to leave."

Soon after we returned home, James left for his new job. Our new stable boy was named Joe Green. He was only fourteen-and-a-half years old, but John thought he would work out all right. One night, John came in and saddled me quickly. My mistress was ill, and we had to go and get the doctor. I galloped faster than I ever had before.

When we reached Dr. White's house, John jumped off and pounded on the door. I was hot and tired, but I still had to take the doctor back to my mistress. John would have to walk back. The doctor was a heavy man, but I did my best, and got him there just in time. As Dr. White hurried inside, Joe Green took me into the stable.

I was dripping wet from running so hard, and my whole body was steaming. Young Joe did his best to cool me off, but he knew very little. He rubbed me down, but did not give me a blanket. He gave me a pail of water that was too cold, but it tasted so good that I drank it all. Then he gave me plenty of oats and corn, and went away, thinking he had done a good job.

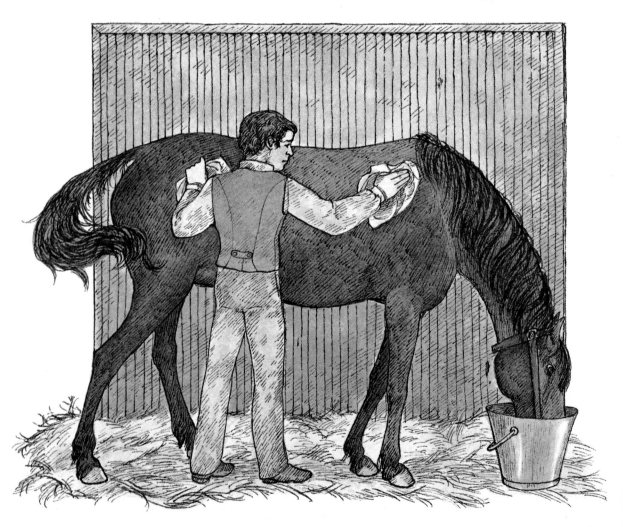

Soon my whole body ached. I was so cold that I trembled. I wanted John, but he was still out on the road, walking back from the doctor's house. When he finally arrived, I was moaning in pain. John knew at once what had happened. He covered me with two or three blankets, and gave me something warm to drink. Finally, I went to sleep.

Joe Green was very upset. But the horse doctor came every day, and I was soon well again. Joe learned quickly, and after a while, John began to trust him with many different chores. One day, Joe and I saw something terrible at the brickyard. A cart was loaded down with heavy bricks, and the driver was cruelly whipping the horses to make them pull it.

They pulled as hard as they could, but the cart was stuck in the mud. Joe called, "I'll help you lighten the load!" But the driver just shouted, "Mind your own business," and kept on whipping the horses. Joe rode off at once, and told the master of the brickyard about the cruel driver. Later, John said that he was proud of Joe for doing what he did.

I lived on the Squire's farm for three years. The mistress was ill from time to time, and the doctor was often sent for. Finally, he said that the best thing for her would be to move to a warmer place. Everyone was sad. Of course, the Squire would have to sell the farm. Now what would happen to us?

We soon found out. The Squire decided that Merrylegs would be given to the minister. Joe Green was to go with the pony and look after him. John Manly said that he would look for a job as a colt-breaker, where he could help young horses get off to a good start. And Ginger and I would have to be sold.

The last day came, and we took the master and mistress to the train. It was a sad day for everyone. But I heard the Squire tell John that Ginger and I had been sold to one of his old friends. "They should be well taken care of," he added. Then, as the train pulled out of the station and disappeared, John jiggled the reins. We were off to our new home.